Hi, Butterfly! by Taro Gomi

William Morrow & Company • New York

Library of Congress Cataloging in Publication Data: Gomi, Taro. Hi, butterfly! Translation of: Kiiroi no wa chōchō. Summary: A young boy chases an elusive butterfly through country fields, city streets, and, even, into his own house. 1. Children's stories, Japanese. [1. Butterflies—Fiction] I. Title. PZ7.G586Hi 1985 [E] 84-1100 ISBN 0-688-04137-X | ISBN 0-688-04138-8 (lib.)

Hi, Butterfly!

Oh, my!

I wish, I hope . . .

Nope!

Cock-a-doodle-doo!

There you go.

Uh-oh!

Got you now.

Whoa . . .

Slow!

Time to go.

What's that?

Splat!

Bye, Butterfly.

Good-bye.